Kiss 2.0

By Angela Clemons

FB: Angela Joy Clemons

IG: Put_God_First_202

IG: i_am_the_greatest_of_my_time

You Tube Channel: Angela Joy Clemons

Put God First Publications

Acknowledgement

I would like to thank the Divine for everlasting love and the gift of life.

Put God First Publications

Kiss 2.0

By Angela Joy Clemons

Introducing Nikolai pronounced Nik-ko-lie born of a Witch and Demon this is his mother Kaitlyn.

Kaitlyn

Kaitlyn was a very powerful

witch, a Descendent from Salem

Virginia, she was born a Witch, her

mother and grandmother were all

witches, they are more powerful

than most Vampires, it is because of

witches that the Vampires even

exist, it was a curse placed

Century's ago, Kaitlyn was very

beautiful she could have any man
she wanted, but all she wanted was
Victor the Vampire hunter, the night
Kaitlyn and Victor got married, he
was bite by a vampire, he had been
trying to kill all year, Victor died in
Kaitlyn arms that night, she refuse
to except this as the end of their
love, so she use black magic to bring
Victor back to life and it worked, or
so she thought. Victor's body had
life in it, but it wasn't him, it was a
powerful demon name Druj a female
demon Goddess of deceit, pain and

manipulation, Archdemon of lies, when Kaitlyn madc lovc and conceived that night it was Nikolai.

Nikolai was born male and female, he possess the spirit of Druj but is human and also has all the power his mother had and more, Druj lives in Nikolai and comes out at least once a month, Nikolai Totally transforms, her whole existence is to ruin the lives of men to cause pain where ever she goes, before she reincarnated totally into Nikolai she use his father to kill many men before killing himself, Kaitlyn knew something wasn't right about her husband once she bought him back, but she just dealt with it, when Nikolai came Kaitlyn was happy again, even though her baby was different, she figured out who it was, but it was nothing she could do, she explained to Nikolai everything and he understood, he grew faster than most kids, he grew in month, by the end of the year he was grown, Kaitlyn let him live his life as he please, and just always

had his back, always watching out
for her baby, she missed Victor so
much and was very lonely, she was
obsessed with Nikolai and would kill
anyone or thing that she thought
was no good for her baby.

Nikolai

Nikolai Smith is half witch half demon, he is also half man half woman, he can be whatever he chooses to be, whenever he chooses to be it. When Nikolai is living as Niko, a Male he has girlfriends and a baby mother, when Nikolai is living as Nikki, she is very dangerous, Nikki is straight psychotic, she can transform into any woman she see and wreaks havoc, where ever, she goes. Nikolai prefers Niko over Nikki, but has the choicc to bc as she or he pleases, Nikolai has a girlfriend name Toni, they have a 3 year old together and Toni is pregnant now with a boy, she knows nothing of Nikolai's other life, she only see's what he want her to see, he loves Toni she is probably the only person other than his mother that he has ever loved, he takes very good care of Toni and the baby, she wants for nothing, as far as she know he is a big time drug dealer and that is ok with her, she loves her life style, so she does and she is told , no questions asked whatever Niko say, that's what Toni do and that's the way he likes it, that's the way he has all his women trained and he has a lot of women but only one baby mother, he plans to marry Toni, Nikolai is very handsome, he is 6'4 brown skin, built with deep waves in his hair, long eye lashes and full lips, he was perfect, there wasn't a woman on the planet that could resist him, and he knew it and played them all,

Nikolai was evil, he destroyed
everything he touch, he has powcr
over Vampires, because of his
mother's genes, he was very special
there was none known like him,
crazy as it may sound that was his
loving side, because his demon side
had no love for humans at all, Nikki
was heartless, ruthless, the devil in
a tight red dress, whenever Nikki
showed up it was to show out, she
has no friends, but Niko has plenty,
his best friend just happens to be
energy Vampire named Thomas, he

is not as powerful as Nikolai, his only power is evil/negative influence over people, like an extreme Narcissist, manipulator, Charmer that also destroys everything he touch and loves every minute of it. Thomas cares for Nikolai, and Nikolai cares for Thomas but he is using Thomas to get at Pastor Matthew Matthews.

Nikolai has many women that he use at will to do whatever he please, he also runs a nonprofit organization called Helping Hands, it's an organization that's gives to the poor and hclp lcss fortunatc families in the community, but it comes at a price, nothing is give, without take with Niko.

Nikolai has an enemy Pastor Matthews; they have hated each other for Century's now and always go back and forth trying to hurt each other. Pastor Matthews is an Original, an old Vampire that cannot be killed, he is the father of most Vampires, well loved and respected by most, his most precious thing in this world is his

wife Brittney Matthews, Nikolai

swore to get Matthew back for

taking his first love Brittney and

with the help of Thomas the plan is

working like a charm, just when

Niko started to get over Brittney he

met Toni who is identical to

Brittney, today is lunch with Sasha

and Thomas.

Sasha and Thomas

So, babe how did last night turn out for you and your girls? Sasha said, it was fantastic, I got too drain the worthless souls of two worthless pieces of shit, one a pedophile and the other a human trafficker, both very proud of their jobs.

Thomas sat there thinking about what he was going to say when she asked how his night went, knowing he was with, Brittney,

Pastor Matthews wife and she was definitely off limits, Sasha would flip her wig, if she knew what Thomas was really up to, so he lied. Sasha, so what did you guys do last night hun? Thomas said, oh nothing much, hit a few strip clubs, shit was dry, my lil homies and I just chilled, remember the 2 youngins I told you about? I gave them some of the purest shit on the streets, opium, I'm not fucking with that crack, so yeah both are hooked, asking for more, so I kindly gave them more. O shit, I almost forgot, I'm supposed to meet Niko at Ruth Chris, he asked about you, I told him, don't even think about it. Sasha said o honey please! Niko and I go way back, he would never, Thomas said, for the record love, I know how far back you go, I have been there your whole life and I don't trust another breathing being, when it come to you, you are more then welcome to come along if you want. Sasha said sure why not, I haven't seen ole Niko since he transforms right before my eyes and started a shot out at the club,

Thomas said what you talking bout

woman? Sasha said I was at the

club Niko was there this was a few

years ago, I thought I told you this

story, so anyway, Niko transformed

into Nikki waited for the girl to leave

him man and Nikki walked right

over to the guy, looking just like the

girl, his girlfriend, she kissed the

man, grabbed his dick and started

grinding on him, of course he

thought it was his girl, drunk and

confused he was just flowing vibing

with Nikki, now the girlfriend comes

back and see Nikki all on her man

looking identical to her, the girl say

"what the fuck is going on here!" the

man just stood there froze put his

hands in the air like, he was under

arrest, but still Nikki was freaking

him down, so the girlfriend snatch

Nikki by her hair but Nikki was too

fast, she beat the shit out the girl,

fucked her whole face up, once they

were pulled apart and the girl friend

noticed what Nikki did to her face

she pulled out a gun and shot in the

air, Nikki disappeared and that was the first time I saw Niko turn into Nikki, when Niko told me what he was, I was just shocked and amazed I never knew a breed existed half witch half demon, so yeah I'm going with you to Ruth Chris to see my old buddy.

Pastor Matthews and Brittney Matthews

Brittney finally woke up after a long night, Pastor was out making a quick run, so she just laid there, thinking about Thomas and the night they spent together, she was wide open and still high off the x-pills he gave her last night, it take at least 3days to get it all out your system, so she closed her eyes, licked her finger and started to rub her clit, thinking of Thomas sucking and licking her all over, she came so hard, she went right back to sleep.

Pastor was supposed to be out making a quick run, he was, a run to Kelly house, getting all kind of ungodly things done to him that his wife would never do, Kelly was licking and sucking the Pastors Anus, which made him weak in the knees, she flipped him over and hummed on his balls before taking both in her mouth while stroking his dick at the same time, she wet his balls up and then swallowed the whole dick, she sucked his dick with

love, wet it up real good and started

softly and slowly at the head and

swallowed it again, sucking at a

rhythm while massaging the balls at

the same time, she made his toes

curl, she sucked him until he

begged her to stop, it was sensitive

now, he couldn't take no more, but

it was still hard, so he bent her over

and solely stroked her from the back

before going all the way in, then

they switch positions, Kelly loved to

ride and she knew this was her

chance to conceive a little Matthew, until she remembered that she is dead and couldn't have kids, so she got on top and stroked his dick like it was all hers, using pussy muscle she didn't know she had, she gripped his dick until he busted all up in her, wishing to God she could have a baby with him, she would have to find another way to trap him in her web.

All the sexual pleasure she brings will be enough to keep her on the Pastors mind, Pastor rolled over kissed Kelly and said two more rounds, thcy both laughcd and laid there a few minutes looking in each other's eyes.

Pastor was reading Kelly thoughts and she had no clue, just as she was thinking "God I love this man" he smiled and kissed her softly and said Pastor I really wish I could do too more rounds love, but I really must go, I have a meeting at the church in 2 hours, I'm going to hit the shower can you fix me something to eat before I go? Kelly said Sure thing baby, what would you like? Pastor said a cold cut with everything on it, Kelly said good choice because I have everything, I need to fix a bomb cold cut, you want fries with it baby? Pastor said Yes love, thank you. Kelly went to the kitchen to get started on her King food, smiling hard feeling like a proud side chick, she fix that cold cut with love for a real king, she went to see if he was finished showering and hadn't even started he was taking a shit, so Kelly got in the shower, he flesh the toilet and joined her and there was round 2 going down, food waiting and Kelly loving every minute.

Pastors phone was ringing off the hook, but pastor didn't see or hear nothing at that moment but Kelly. It was one of the old nosey church members calling to tell Pastor that she seen Brittney last night with a man at a very expensive Hotel, but then she hung up, because she would have to tell what she was doing at that very expensive hotel, and how she didn't see Brittney with him, but she seen her go in the same room the gentlemen went in and they were in there for hours, and how she saw Brittney leaving because she was leaving at the same time, but she never really saw Brittney with anyone for sure. This fair lady name is Stacy and she attends Pastors Church, she is also one of Nikolai women, she does whatever he tells her to do, so he told her to befriend Brittney, Stacy decided to call Brittney, Brittney answered the phone Hello, Stacy

said hello this is Stacy I attcnd your

church and was given your number

for counsel, Brittney said ok how

can I help you love? Better yet just

meet me at the church today at 4,

what's your last name so I can tell

my staff I am expecting you,

Queenstown, Stacey Queenstown.

Brittney got up hit the shower and

started her day, which was half gone

she looked at the clock 2:15 pm

wow I have slept most of the day

away thinking to herself, where is

my husband so she called Pastor, but it went straight to voice mail, which was not like him, he answered when she called no matter what, she thought umm? Naw?! Got in her car and headed for the church.

Pastor finally made it to church, 10 mins late because of Kelly, He walked in 2min before Brittney walked in, and Stacy Queenstown walked in right after Brittney, headed for Brittney's office, as soon as she was about to knock on the door Brittney opened it and surpriscd thcm both, facc to face Stacey said Hello Mrs. Matthews I'm Stacey Queenstown, We spoke earlier today, Brittney said O yes I remember dear, I was just on my way to the kitchen for coffee would you like a cup? Come on walk with me. Brittney and Stacy were on their way to the kitchen , and ran right into Pastor coming out his office, hello Husband Brittney said he kissed Brittney, this is Stacey Queenstown she is here for a council session today, that's great

babe, on my way to another

meeting, see you later today love

said Pastor, ok I love you said

Brittney, Pastor was on his way to a

meeting about the homeless, it was

asked by the people that the

homeless be allowed to sleep in the

church at night during the week and

give them breakfast and prayer in

the morning at 9 am every morning,

Pastor thought it was a great idea,

so he wanted to meet with the

congregation to see if they agree

with what he wanted to do, even though he already decided that it was what he was going to do anyway regardless of what everyone thought but wanted to be considerate and let everyone know what was about to take place.

Brittney and Stacey entered her office so they could begin counsel, Stacey knowing her intentions are no good , had to come up with a good story to tell Brittney, a story that would be all lies of course, something that could get her in and make Brittney feel sorry for her, she wanted Niko to be proud of her, so she put on her best hurt face. Brittney looked at Stacey and said so how can I help you dear? Stacey begin her lie she said I'm in an abusive relationship, I'm married to a man that beats me when I don't do what he ask me to do, I'm at a point in my life where I need change before he kill me or I kill him! Brittney said o my goodness, how long have you been in this relationship? 2 years said Stacey,

Brittney said ok Stacey if you are ready to leave him, we can put you in a safe house until we get you situated, Stacey said safe house? Let me think about it, I'm staying with my sister right now, I'm not in immediate danger, but I do need to cut ties. Brittney said ok let me know what you want to do dear, Brittney phone notification went off she got a text, it was Thomas saying " love you my beautiful Queen" she smiled and put the phone in her pocket, Stacey just looked at her wondering who or what it was that made her smile, they got up so Brittney could walk Stacey out, once at the door she hug Stacey and said call me if you need to talk or need to get away, be strong everything will be ok.

The congregation sat waiting for Pastor to join them and get the meeting started, he just got a text from Kelly it was a picture of her pleasing herself the text said "Patiently waiting" he smiled, his dick got hard, he put his phone in his pocket and begin to speak,

Thank you all for being in

attendance today, I want to talk

about a huge change, I will be

bringing forth in the church. I want

to let the homeless sleep in the

church at night in the isles, we will

supply food and blankets, they will

be able to enter at 7pm and have to

be out by 9am Monday through

Friday, we will also help them get

their lives together, those that want

to, and those, that are willing, we

will offer counsel and job training,

so what do you think? Everyone was quite for a minute and then Ms. Edith spoke she said Pastor I think you are a good man with a good heart, but I don't want nothing to do with no dirty homeless people, they drug addicts and murderers they dirty and carry lice, so if they sleeping in the church, who is going to clean the church up after these people? I feel that you are putting us good clean Christian people at risk Pastor, I love you and support you but not on this I must vote no! The

Pastor just smiled and looked at

Edith already knowing she would be

the one to speak out, Pastor said

Ms. Edith I understand your

concern dear bless your heart, but

this is not a matter that will be

debated or voted on this is a matter

that will be! Because I decided it will

be, so you all will help with the

operation of this task this is our

mission and so we will all clean the

church and help as many people, as

we possibly can, is there anyone else

that would like to speak? If not the

meeting is over, we will meet again on Friday and begin service, get the word out there please and thank you in advance, everyone got up to leave, Ms. Edith stormed out so mad she left the church for the rest of the evening, Pastor was the last one to leave.

Pastor was headed to Brittney's office, he entered but she wasn't there he looked at the notes on her desk that read "Stacey Queenstown Possible safe house stay, abusive relationship" he thought to his self "who the fuck is this bitch" then took out his phone to call his wife, but she was coming though the office door, they kissed, closed the door, he lifted up her dress and started sucking her breast, he pulled her panties off and sucked her pussy wetting it up real good before bending her over the desk going in real deep, Pastor's dick was not as big as Thomas, so when he entered her he felt the difference immediately, he also noticed a smelled he has never smelled before coming from his wife, his dick went

soft and he pulled out, knowing

deep down inside, that somebody

parked in his garage and it was

nothing she could possibly say that

would make him believe otherwise,

Brittney pussy was always tight and

smelled just like him, what he just

felt was super loose, it did not fit

like a glove, the grip wasn't right

and the smell was way off, it made

him angry he knew that the best

thing for him to do right now was to

get away from her and go process

the information before he choked her to death, he pulled his pants up and left out the door, leaving her bent over the desk ass showing wondering what just happen. She fixed her clothes and went to the bath room to clean herself up, and noticed the smell herself, a very foul odor, she thought to herself " what the fuck" she left the church and went straight to the doctor office, but it was packed so she was given an appoint for the 8 am as soon as they open, not satisfied with the

outcome she went to CVS to get a
medicated douche, she went home
and got in the bath tub, before she
inserted the douche something told
her to stick her fingers up there and
she did, she felt something in her
vagina, she pulled out a condom
that Thomas had used and left
inside her, so also caught an
infection from him fucking her in
the ass and going straight to the
vagina, bacteria, Brittney was so
green, she had no idea what was
going on with her vagina, she would

Put God First Publications

have to wait for tomorrow and face

her husband tonight, Brittncy was a

kind sweet, innocent good girl and

pastor was her first real love she has

never been with anyone other than

Pastor, Thomas was the second man

Brittney has ever been with

sexually, right now Brittney felt like

she needed counseling so she called

Sasha, because she couldn't think

of another person to call that she

could trust to talk about her life and

problems. Brittney had no idea what

she had got herself into and what

47

she was going to do, she didn't want to face her husband and was thinking of asking Sasha could she stay with her for the night. She called her husband praying that he didn't answer and he didn't it went straight to voice mail, so she knew he didn't want to talk, because he never sent her to voice mail, Brittney sat there thinking crying, confused, sorry and then she got a text from Thomas it was a dick pic saying" he all yours baby meet me tonight" she smiled then thought to herself girl you are losing your

mind.

Tina

Tina was lying in bed with her boyfriend's best friend, her boyfriend had just left for work, and his friend just happen to stop by to pick up his phone he left last night, Marco knew that Rick was coming to get the phone so he left it with his girl Tina, and told her "Rick coming to get his phone give him the phone and don't let him in" Tina said ok. When Rick knocked on the door, Tina opened the door and let him in, she said wait here, the phone is in

the kitchen I will get it for you, Tina

standing there in only a wifebeater

and G-string, he watched her walk

to the kitchen and back, she said

silly me it's not in the kitchen, it's in

the room, she walked towards the

room he followed, once in the room

she bent over to pick the phone up

off the floor, she turned around to

give it to him and he pushed her on

the bed, taking off his shirt and

dropping his sweat pants. They

fucked in the bed she shares every

night with Marco feeling no guilt,

loving every minute. Her phone was

ringing off the hook and had been

for the last 15 minutes, but she

never noticed because she was too

busy showing out for Rick, it was

Marco calling back to back because

he didn't trust her and knew for

sure that Rick was scum and would

try to fuck his girl, he did it before,

so Marco was damn near having an

anxiety attack, he told his Boss, he

had an emergency and had to pick

up his son from school early, his

Boss told him he had one hour to take care of his business and get back, Marco said cool and got in his truck headed for his apartment with all kind of crazy thoughts running thought his mind, once he reached his destination and realized Rick's car was still parked outside, he was seeing red and Tina still wasn't answering her phone, he walked right in the door wasn't even locked, Rick nor Tina locked it before going in the room, Marco entered the apartment and just stood there for a second listening, he didn't hear

anything at first, he opened the

room door and there was Tina

sucking Rick dick, while he was laid

back on the bed with his eyes

closed, Marco hit Tina so hard she

almost bit Rick dick clean off, he hit

her again and broke her neck or so

he thought, Rick passed out half his

dick was gone. Marco was standing

there trying to process what just

happen and what to do next, then

Tina jumped up and snapped her

neck back in place, Marco couldn't

believe his eyes, he ran out his own

apartment and went back to work.

Tina got herself together and called

the ambulance for Rick, she texted

Marco and said "its ok baby come

back home I'm sorry" Marco looked

at the text and text back "wtf, are

you? Tina replied a demon now

what? I'm not going to kill you

Marco I love you, Marco text back

"wtf is Rick?" Tina text back "at the

hospital he ok" Marco text back "get

the fuck out my apartment we are

done! Its over bitch!" Tina Text back

"we done when I say when done, I
will see you tonight" Tina had Marco
scared as shit and Marco wasn't
scared of nothing. He text back " I'm
coming home with the cops, now
leave, he felt like a bitch writing that
text, but this aint no regular bitch,
this bitch died and came back to life
right in front of him, he sat there
thinking fuck that! I'm not even
going back to that apartment! Man,
what the fuckkkk!!!!, I need to talk
so he called his good friend Niko.
Marco was shook for the first time in

his life he didn't know what to do,

Tina put her clothes on and left the

apartment leaving the key behind

she was done wit Marco, on her way

to her other boyfriend apartment

Lovail, she knocked on the door and

a female opened it, Tina said Who

the fuck are you! The women replied

Lovail's sister who the fuck is you!

Tina said o shit Lisa?! I'm sorry poo,

he did tell me you were coming over,

I apologize, I'm Tina his soon to be

wife and your sister, Lisa said yes I

know who you are, he can't stop

talking about you, come on in sister.
Tina said I so apologize for going on
you like that please forgive me,
Lovail told me all about you but
never showed me a picture, so when
I see this beautiful woman open the
door, Lisa said I understand, I get it,
I kind of figured you would react like
that and I must admit I wanted to
mess with you a little to see where
your crazy was at, Tina said well
you got me good, out walks Lovail,
he kissed Tina and said so what you
think sis she hot or not? Lisa said o

she definite hot, superhot bro, you
got a sister? Yes I am gay, Lovail
said Lisa don't start that shit, she
off limits, she not one of my
playthings so don't try to fuck my
girl, let me just put that out there
for all to hear, because I'm not
playing no games bout this one, Lisa
said bro I'm not messing wit you I
heard you loud and clear, this one a
keeper got you, I got a girl anyway
and I'm happy for you, never
thought it would happen being the
gigolo that you are, Lovail said I'm

not a gigolo playa yes gigolo no!

there is a difference, I have never

used a woman for money, for pussy

yes money no, and I'm done now,

right baby? Tina said Hell yeah! You

belong to me and me only, I will kill

a bitch over you, real live jack! You

hear that, until death do us part

baby, she kissed him real sloppy

and nasty. Lisa said yuck save that

shit for when I leave, I need to talk

to your bro about something real

important, Lovail said what is it sis?

You can talk in front of her I trust

her, Lisa said well I wanna know

how we, you and I became the way

we are today? Lovail said well sister

we are half human and half witch

we can have kids, but we are

possessed by an evil demon that

was placed upon us at birth, our

mother was an evil witch that fell in

love with a human and we are her

karma, mother cannot die, she is

cursed and so are we, Lisa said but

brother I want to do right, I no

longer desire to in flick pain and

misery on people I want to be

happy, I'm sick Lovail I need help.

Lovail said sis nothing can help you,

you have to help you, you must

learn to control your thoughts, focus

on positive instead of negative, it

will be extremely hard but it is

imperative, you must find balance if

you want to learn to use all your

powers. Lisa said ok I hear you bro,

well I have to go see mother I will

call you later, and I need to stay the

night, I don't want to be alone right

now, Lovail hugged his sister and

said that fine sis, here is a spare key

incase I'm not here, Lisa said

thanks bro, Tina it was a pleasure

meeting you hope you here tonight

so we can have sister time, I need it,

tina said ok babe I will be here and

everything will be fine love she

hugged Lisa and Lisa left. Tina said

so that baby sis. Lovail said yeah

that's her, he kissed her again,

where have you been, I was calling

like a crazy man? Tina said o babe

was at the church you know my

father Jesus come first, Lovail said

Tina who the fuck you think you

playing with woman?! Now you don't know but you will learn that I am the master of destruction, we are two of a kind, let's go in this room and you can tell me all about your no good deeds, Tina said I love you so much, my twin soul, Lovail said baby I just stop starting shit, I will tell you all about it, the last shit I did that made me want to do good, so I'm locked up over dc jail, I hear this nigga name Tank say he would kill my bitch ass, right? So, bam! I took the book Rich had and Rich was this big bully terrifying

muthfucker that nobody fuckcd with

he was to big 7 feet 400 pounds

nobody fuck wit big Rich and he was

on butt, so I put the book right in

Tank cell on his bunk, Big Rich

come out the shower looking for his

book, now he has told the whole

unit don't touch his book, so when

he go to his cell to get his book and

its gone, he flip the fuck out, he say

whoever got my book I'm breaking

your face, everybody sitting quite

looking at this big nigga flip out all

wondering who the fuck got his

book, he going cell to cell check

everybody shit and aint nobody

saying nothing, he get to Tank cell

and see his book on Tank bed, he

roars Tankkkkk!!!! What the fuck

you doing with my book! Tank

turned around and said man what

the fuck you talking bout! I aint

touch your book! Big rich rush

Tank, it wasn't nothing Tank could

do Rich was just too Big, he broke

his face just like he said he would.

Tina sat listening to his story she

said wow that was wicked but not

evil, let me tell you a cvil wickcd

story, as a matter of fact this just

happen, she begin to tell him about

Marco and Rick and how she may

need him to put hands on Marco,

Lovail said damn babe he broke

your neck and you bit Rick dick off,

she said yes, he said yeah you got

me lord have mercy, girl take them

clothes off, lets fuck, I'm not making

love to you right now I wanna fuck

you, I'm about to choke you while

hitting you from the back until you

pass out then imma smack you

back to life, Tina said let's do it, as

long as I get to fuck you in the ass

with my 9 inch dildo, he said bet let

the fun begin.

Nikolai

Thomas/Sasha (the lunch date)

Thomas and Sasha were already seated when Nikolai walked in to Ruth Chris with all eyes on him, you would think he was a movie star, he greeted them and they all sat, Nikolai said Thomas it is good to see you brother and always a pleasure to be in your presence Sasha, Thomas I called you here today because I am starting a massage service in the DC area with all the gentrification that

has taken place the money is now

plentiful, I want you to run it

Thomas and I would love for you to

manage it Sasha, I have 10 girls all

certified massage specialist ready to

work, I just found the perfect

location and its under construction

as we speak, will be ready in 2

weeks, so what do you say, are you

in? Sasha said hell yeah! I'm in

sounds like fun, Thomas said count

me in too Boss, just then Sasha

phone rang it was Kelly, asking

Sasha to come get her she wanted to

hang, she told Kelly shc would be

there in a hour, she then said to the

guys, I must run that was Kelly she

needs me, I'm not that hungry

anyway, you to catch up, honey I

will see you later, Nikolai always

good to see you, looking forward to

our new business venture, she got

up and left the restaurant, Niko

waited until she was completely

gone before he spoke to Thomas

about the real reason for the

meeting. Nikolai said to Thomas, so

how is everything going with

Brittney? Thomas said according to

plan, I took her places she has never

been before, X- pills, Dope, Crack,

Drink, I told her to meet me later, I

need to go check on my youngins

real quick, ride wit me? Nikolai said

cool let's go. They stopped at the

carry out for some roll ups and

chicken wings covered in mumbo

sauce, it was to thots in their giving

it all the way up, ass out tiddys out,

Niko and Thomas just looked at

each other and smiled, Niko said to

the brown skin girl, hello love, I'm

Niko this is my partner Johnny,

what's you and your friend names?

What yall boutta get into? She said

I'm Sophia and that's Larissa and

we about to get into whatever yall

boutta get into! Niko said cool how

old are you love? Sophia lied and

said I'm 18 and Larissa 19, knowing

damn well they are both 15. The

girls got their food, Niko got his

food, paid for everybody food.

Johnny called Dre to see if they were

home, they were, so he told Dre he

was on his way and has a few

friends with him, Dre said cool.

They all got in Thomas aka Johnny

truck and went to Dre house,

Johnny knocked, and Jose opened

the door very happy to see J,

because they were almost out of

drugs, they stop selling and became

straight users. Johnny, Niko Sophia

and Larissa all entered and sat in

the living room, J introduced

everyone and turned the tv on You

Tube videos Migos, he pulled out

some pure dope and put lines on the

table, the girls faking pretending like

they know, what they are doing

based off TV, first they watch Dre

take a dollar bill and snort a whole

line, Sophia tried to do what he did

and passed out, it hit her head so

hard, Dre told Larissa don't snort

the whole line, he gave her a one on

one, she was high floating, Sophia

came to and was now floating along

feeling good as well, Jose snorted a

line while Niko and just watched

then passed around a baseball bat J

filled with loud bubble gum Kush

the best shit out at the time, J made

everybody a drink and the party

begin, Larissa got up and started

dancing then stripping, Sophia got

up and joined in the entertainment,

Dre got up and started dancing with

the girls, while Jose just sat there

jealous rolling his eyes, but he

knows Dre expects him to play it off

at all times, so he got with the

program and got up and dance with

them, he pulled Sophia to him and

started feeling all over her while Dre

was humping Larissa. Niko and

Johnny got up to leave, he left

enough pure for the whole

neighborhood, he told the boys he

would hit them later and gave the

girls money to catch a ride home.

Brittney and Sasha

Sasha was on her way to pick up
Kelly when Brittney called, hello
said Sasha, hi this is Brittney are
you busy right now can you talk?
Sasha said well right now I am
driving, I can call you back in about
an hour, Brittney said ok and hung
up just as Sasha was pulling up to
Kelly's. Sasha parked and got out to
go in, she entered Kelly's place,
Kelly was smiling happy to see her,
hey girly said Kelly, you are glowing

bitch! What's that pastor dick in your guts? Kelly said you know it! He is not as big as I like but, he knows what to do with what he got. Tina and rolled her eyes in the air, guess who just called me to talk? Who Sasha? Said Kelly, Brittney said Sasha, for what, what she thinks yall friends? Said Kelly. Well pastor is my dad, so I must pretend to like her even if I don't said Sasha. Kelly said well I sucked your daddy dry this morning and plan to do it again tonight, yuck said Sasha have you talk to Tina? Kelly said no call

her, so Sasha called, and Tina

answered, Tina where you at hoe?

Come over to Kelly's, Tina said cool

on my way now. Brittney sat in her

car trying to get her thoughts

together, she called Matthew again

and again it went straight to voice

mail, Pastor was at the bar drinking,

something he has not done in years,

ignoring Brittney calls, trying to

figure out what he wanted to do, he

decided to do nothing, play it cool

the truth will come out, it always

does, who? Is what he wants to know most of all, who is the man crazy enough to disrespect him, knowing he would kill them and at that very moment in walk Niko and Johnny, he looked up and saw Niko and a feeling went through him, he knew at that moment Niko had something to do with it, but why was he with Thomas was now his question and where did he fit in, he hated Niko and would not miss the chance to kill him if given, he got up and left the bar before he did something reckless.

Brittney knew she fucked up, so she just went home and ran another bath just to soak and try to figure out what next, and if calling Sasha was the right thing to do. She got out the tub put on her night clothes then her phone rang, it was Thomas, Hello handsome Brittney said, I miss you Thomas said looking in pastors direction as he was leaving the bar, I love you B just called to tell you that and I will call you tomorrow good night,

goodnight Thomas I love you to, she

hung up and just that fast she

forgot all about Pastor, her phone

rang again, this time it was Stacey,

Hello said Brittney, Hi it's me Stacey

jut called to see if you wanted to go

to a poetry jam with me tomorrow

from 3pm to 6pm called Heart of a

Poet poetry Jam by Angela joy

Clemons, Brittney said sure Stacey I

would love too, thank you for

thinking of me and for the invite, see

you tomorrow at 3, are things ok

with you? Yes, I'm good for the time

being said Stacey, see you

tomorrow.

Pastor/Nikolia/Thomas

Pastor sat in his truck thinking, he knew it was one of the two, yes he hated Nikolai and he knew Nikolai hated him, but he also knows Nikolai is no fool, Nikolai knows that pastor would kill him and every relative he has living, Thomas on the other hand is naïve and cocky, Pastor got out his truck and walked back into the bar right over to Niko and Thomas aka Johnny, Niko seen him coming and knows of his power to read minds, to see into your life past present and future, he also

knows pastor is deadly and would

not hesitate to kill him, that's why

he put Thomas up to do his dirty

work. Niko said to Thomas do not

shake his hand, before he could say

why, pastor was standing right there

in front of them he spoke first,

Pastor said Nikolai it has been a

long time, when did you come back

to DC? Who is your friend? Niko

said I have been back about a year

now, this is Johnny. Pastor

extended his hand, Thomas shook it

his hand anyway after Niko told him

not to, pastor smiled at Thomas and

said Thomas I didn't even recognize

you, guess I had to many drinks,

you are dating my daughter Sasha

correct? Yes, Thomas said, take it

easy fellas Pastor said as he walked

away, making plans to kill Niko and

Thomas. Niko said to Thomas I told

you not to shake his hand! The

nigga can see into your life past

present and future, Thomas smiled,

Niko what the fuck you smiling for,

you shook his hand believe me he

knows, and he will come for you

guaranteed! Thomas, said Niko are

you scared of Pastor? Because I'm

not worried at all about him, I just

don't want Sasha to find out

anything. Just then Stacey and

Edith walked into the bar, they

asked playfully if the seated next to

them were taken? Then Stacey

kissed Niko and Edith introduced

herself to Johnny and said to him,

haven't I seen you at church with

sister Sasha? Johnny replied yes

that is my wife, o ok how is she

doing? She is great blessed and highly favored said Johnny, how about us taking this party somewhere else ladies? Let's go said Edith. Pastor sat in his truck watching the bar, he watched as Niko, Johnny, Edith and Stacey exited and got in Johnny truck, dead men walking he thought to himself and pulled off. He called Sasha and asked where she was he needed to talk, now Sasha is sitting there wondering what's going on, Brittney called earlier now he calling, she said pops I'm over Kelly house come on over she would not mind at all. On my way said Pastor. Niko and Thomas took Stacey and Edith to a hotel where they fucked them both and got them high as the sky.

Pastor and Sasha

Pastor Matthews used his key to enter Kelly's apartment, not hiding the fact that he was her guy, the girls were in the living room chilling, laughing, looking at Love and Go-go, a DC reality show produced by Angela Joy Clemons, starring female rapper Dark angel, he came in spoke to everyone and sat there quite for a minute, he sipped his drink, got up to add more ice, rolled his own J of loud, he puffed it a few times, sipped his drink, looked at Sasha and said I love you, you know this, I would never do anything to hurt you, I loved your mother many centuries ago, but Thomas/Johnny whatever his name is, he is a dead man walking, I am going to kill him Sasha, him and his buddy Nikolai are as good as dead, Thomas is fucking Brittney! Sasha looked shock, she was at a loss for words, she couldn't believe what she was hearing, but she knew it had to be truth coming from her father, he was a very serious man. Kelly said

How did you find out. Pastor said I

fucked Brittney earlier today in her

office, her pussy was loose and had

an odor, I been fucking her for the

last 10 years and it has never been

loose or had an odor. So I went to

the bar to have a few drinks and

clear my mind, as I am sitting there

thinking of who could be so insane

as to disrespect me in this way

knowing I will kill them and

everybody related to them, and in

walks Nikolai and Thomas a feeling

shot through me, I can't even explain, I left the bar before I did something I would regret and went to my truck, I sat there a few minutes, then I went back in to speak to him and see what I feel, I shook Thomas hand who he introduced to me as Johnny, and when I shook his hand I could see everything in his life past present future, I saw him fucking Brittney, so it is nothing he could say, she could say, its nothing anyone can do to change what is, what am I going to do to Brittney you are probably

wondering, well, I don't know yet,

but those two fools are as good as

dead. I will take the souls from the

soulless, matter of fact how and

when is the question at hand, Sasha

I know you love him and I know this

news is not easy for you, but

daughter he must be taught a

lesson. Sasha said I understand

father, but please spare his life, beat

him almost dead, blind him even

but don't kill him please father

please, Sasha got up and left crying

uncontrollably, Tina got up and ran

after her, Kelly went to comfort

pastor with some Sloppy, noisy head

she sucked his balls and deep

throated his dick, biting his thighs

before she licked and sucked his ass

hole, he felt faint, he never had his

ass ate and sucked before, she got

on top of him using her pussy

muscles she stroked slow and at a

rhythm, he came so hard he went

straight to sleep, Kelly went to take

a bubble bath, then prepared lunch

for Pastor when he woke up.

Sasha/Thomas/Nikolai

Thomas dropped Niko off at

one of his women's apartment on

the south side, Woodland, then

headed home, he called Sasha but it

went straight to voice mail, so he

called back again, still no answer,

he was now home, he entered looked

around for his wife, she wasn't

there, so he made a drink and just

sat and waited on Sasha, he could

feel something wasn't right, Sasha

walked in the apartment and went

straight to the room, without

speaking or even looking at Thomas, he followed her asking what's wrong my love? She looked at him and begin to cry, why Thomas? Of all the women in the world you have my permission to fuck! You fuck Brittney Matthews! After I told you she was off limits and that my father is obsessed with the bitch! He is going to kill you Thomas and there is nothing I can do to stop him. You are Nikolai are dead men walking, Nikolai used you to touch my father, you see Nikolai was in love with

Brittney but my father took her from
him, and they have been enemy's
ever since, Nikolai knows he is not
stronger then my father, he knows
that my father is looking for a
reason to kill him just because, I
don't know what to say or feel right
now, I just wanna run away.
Thomas said well babe, I'm sorry
but not sorry, let's leave now and
come back in a few years, Sasha
said you can't run from him Thomas
he knows all and will find us, I'm
not running, I'm not going out

without a fight, Thomas called Niko
he knows Sasha said he is going to
kill us, Niko said I told you, all
because you shook his hand, damn
fool, I'm leaving I suggest you do the
same. I'm not running she won't let
me, guess I gotta face this shit head
on. Niko said well thanks for letting
me know what I already knew, I'm
out and I will check up on you in a
few years' peace. Niko was sitting in
his car and immediately
transformed into Nikki, headed for
ATL leaving behind his girl and kids,

a decision he would surly regret. He called Toni and told her he loved her and the kids, and would come back for her once he figured out his next move, he told her he fucked up and had to run to save his life, but he promised to send money and come back for her, just then it was a knock at the door, a special knock, Toni opened the door and standing in front of her was Pastor Matthew Matthews.

<u>Pastor's Revenge</u>

Pastor talked to Kelly for a while, his phone beeped it was Sasha she text him "father I love you, but I must run away with Thomas, I can't allow you to kill my one true love, please don't hate me, please don't look for us, I will never come back to DC unless you request, father please understand" Pastor said to Kelly Sasha is running off with Thomas! She just saved his life; they better be leaving the united states that's the only

hope for his ass! I will call you later

love, he kissed Kelly and left, Pastor

got in his truck headed for Toni's

place, that's Niko's baby-mother he

thought no one knew about, Pastor

knocked on the door and was

shocked when Toni answered the

door, she was identical to Brittney,

he thought to himself Toni and

Brittney had to be twins separated

at birth, he fell in love instantly, he

just stood there looking at her. Can

I help you sir? Said Toni, I'm sorry

love said Pastor, I'm Matt Niko sent

me to help you while he is away, he

didn't tell me you were pregnant,

come in Toni said, I need to sit

down, boy or girl Pastor asked girl

said Toni can I touch your stomach

Pastor asked yes said Toni, Pastor

touched her stomach and made her

go into labor right there, he took her

to the hospital and stayed right

there by her side through the whole

birth, he even sent Niko pictures of

him holding his new born baby girl.

Pastor kissed Toni on her forehead

and told her he would be back

tomorrow to get her and the baby,

he told her she could live with him

rent free and he would take care of

her. Pastor pulled in his driveway

and just sat thinking of how he

would deal with Brittney, he

couldn't bring his self to kill her, he

got out and went inside, she was

standing there waiting, all of the

drugs were out her system by now,

so she was seeing things a little

more cleared then before, she

dropped to her knees begging Pastor

for forgiveness, pastor told her to get

up, he looked her in the eyes and

took her hand and they went

upstairs, he ran bath water for her

and told her to get in, she did as

told, under a spell she told nothing

but solid truth, he looked her in the

eyes and said sternly, if you ever

disrespect me again in any way I will

kill you! Then he put her head

under the water until she almost

drown, he let her up just in time,

and left her there, he got in bed, she

came to bed dressed sexy, he wasn't

interested he told her, we will be

having a house guest, her name is

Toni and she has a new born baby

girl coming with her and a 3year old

coming along as well, goodnight

Brittney. The next day Brittney got

her test results back from the

hospital, she was pregnant and had

a bacterial infection, all she heard

was pregnant, how was she going to

explain this to Pastor, she started

crying, sitting in her office waiting

on Stacey for their 2nd counsel

session, in walked Stacey she asked

Brittney what was wrong and Brittney broke down and told her everything that happen, now Brittney felt like she wanted revenge and like Stacey was counseling her.

Pastor went to pick Toni up from the hospital he took them to their new home, his house, he gave Toni one of his cars to drive and she had her own room, he also gave her a weekly allowance of 2,000 Toni was in heaven she didn't think twice about Niko after she called and the phone was disconnected she let it go and got in tuned with her new life with Pastor. Brittney walk in her house with Stacey right behind her, pastor and Toni were in the family room with the baby looking like a big happy family, Brittney couldn't believe her eyes it was her twin sister Whitney, who changed her name to Toni and left the family many years ago because she hated being a twin, they never got along because of Toni's jealousy, Toni always felt that their parents treated Brittney better because she was the good one that did what she was told

and followed the rules, Whitney

hated Brittney and Brittney hated

her as well. What the fuck are you

doing in my house with my husband

bitch! Brittney said to Toni, Toni

smiled when she looked up and seen

her twin furious, you see Pastor told

Toni the whole story so she knew

exactly what was going on, Toni said

to Brittney I live here now, this is

my new home sissy, your husband

is the god father to my kids my

sponsor and life coach, I see you

still hang with trash, Pastor Stacey

is not wanted here please ask her to

leave our home, trash is not

allowed. Stacey said fuck you bitch;

Niko don't want your ass! That's

why he left you hoe! I will leave

willingly bitch! Call me when you

need me Brittney, I got your back,

she hugged Brittney and left. Pastor

said Toni, Brittney, real twins, I am

the luckiest man in the world, I'm

talking planet earth, I got two

beautiful loves for letting them live,

for now any way, not bad, I'm not

even mad at Nikolai no more, Pastor

was smiling looking at them, then

Brittney stood up and said I'm

pregnant! And walked up the steps,

leaving that taste in his mouth, the

whole time thinking it was Thomas

baby but it wasn't it was Pastors, he

went to a witch doctor not too long

ago for help to bring forth a child

with his wife unbeknown to her,

what the witch doctor gave him

worked , because Brittney was

pregnant and it was for sure Pastors

baby, Brittney would find out soon

enough, she was streaming seeing

her sister in her house and this new

living arrangement Pastor has

pulled on her, she lay there

wondering who baby it was, because

her and pastor had been trying all

year fucking like they were teen

agers, but she knew she had fucked

Niko and the condom was in her so

she just prayed it was her husband

baby, she called Stacey to help her

come up with a plan to get rid of her

twin sister, she even thought of

killing her, how did this all go so wrong so fast, lord help me please.

Pastor kissed Toni on the forehead and said he would be back, he was going to the church for a second to make sure everything was going as planed with the homeless mission, he left feeling like a new man. Once he arrived at the church, he saw a line outside and asked someone why the lined-up, someone pointed at Edith, Edith! Pastor said what's going on here?! Edith said I am only letting in women and kids for the

first hour! Pastor snapped he said
you fucking, whoring, drug addict
bitch who the fuck is you to change
the rules and try to regulate shit! I
said everybody man woman and
child, let these people in! you not
running shit, you better hope and
pray that you are never in this
predicament, now get the fuck outta
here! Yall come on he said to the
people it was cold as shit outside at
the time, he held the door open for
the people to enter, he noticed a lot

of young people, probably addicted

to something lost and confused.

Tina/ Lovail / Lisa

Lovail was at the studio, while Tina and Lisa was at his place smoking and chilling, Lisa's new friend Stacey came over and she bought her friend Edith with her, the ladies got lit and had fun, first Stacey and Lisa started making out and of course tina and Edith followed, so it looked like one big orgy going on in the middle of Lovail's living room. Lovail walked in with his homie Say-Say. Both shocked at what was going on right

in front of them, it didn't take long

for the guys to get naked and join,

Tina and Edith were all over Lovail,

Lisa and Stacey made Say-Say cry,

Lisa was licking his ass while Stacey

was sucking his toes, Tina sat on

Lovail face while Edith sucked his

dick balls and all, they suck licked

and fucked for about an hour. They

took a break, rolled up, pop a e-pill

and started all over again, Tina

thought to herself these are the

coolest muthfuckers on the planet,

her phone rang it was Sasha but
she didn't answer, so Sasha texted
her " Pastor is trying to kill Thomas
so I have run away with him. Never
to return, I love you, wish me well
sis". Tina called Kelly to see if this
was real, if she really ran off with
him, Kelly confirmed it she was
gone, she had so much more gossip
about Brittney, Toni the new baby
and the pregnancy Tina was at a
loss for words.

Nikolai's Revenge

Nikolai was driving when he received the text from Pastor of him with Toni and Nikolai's new baby girl, he had to pull over, he was so mad he almost hit the car in front of him, he was two blocks away from his whore name Bianca house, so he stop by to get his self together, he called to let her know he was stopping by, so she would have everything together, meaning any niggas, her place was the spot, once he got there he walked right in, and

she was sitting at her card table

with two friends smoking and

drinking, while her kids ran around

destroying the house, Bianca had 7

kids by 7 men, her oldest sons

Gucci and Versace were torturing

the cat, while her daughters were

watching stripper videos practicing,

her youngest daughter Barbie aka

shit-shit was sitting in her high

chair shitty, her friend Mia got up to

get some more drink and smelled

shit- shit, she said to Bianca girl

your daughter is shitty change her please, why yall call her shit-shit anyway? Bianca said because her father some shit and all she does is shit; she will be alright 'Lexus come change your sister!" Bianca hollered in the next room for her oldest daughter to come change her youngest daughter, but she never responded leaving shit-shit sitting in shit. Niko just stood there for a minute watching the whole scene play out, thinking this bitch is trifling, Bianca picked up shit-shit and walk towards her room telling

Niko to come on, once in the room

he sat on the bed, she said what's

up boo? She put shit-shit on the bed

took the pamper off and went to get

the wipes, by the time she came

back bed bugs was all over shit-shit,

Niko looked at the baby and was like

Aye Yo! What the fuck! He jumped

up off the bed he was sitting on, he

said let me get the fuck outta here!

Imma holla at you slim and left,

shaking his clothes off, thinking"

this bitch is discussing, I aint never

seen a mothfucker live so nasty" he got in his car and drove right pass ATL, he went to New Orleans to his mom, he needed her, he wanted to kill Matthew and if anybody could help him it would be her the only person he trusted in the world his mother. Nikolai knocked on the door, standing there with a big smile, Kaitlyn open the door to a beautiful surprise, she grabbed him kissing him all over his face like a kid, My Nikolai she said looking him in his eyes reading what he has been through, aww my baby come

lct mothcr hcal you son, let's talk,

Mother Nikolai said "he took her

mother! He took Toni and my baby"

I need you to help me kill him

mother, Son it would take all I am to

go up against Matthew Matthews,

I'm not willing to do that son, but I

will help you get revenge. How? Said

Nikolai, Matthew has a brother and

sisters he takes care of to this day,

many centuries ago they died and

he had a spell cast to bring them

back to life, but they have no power,

before they died they had kids, so

his human decedents are living right

here, his brothers Mark and Mike

Matthews are here his sister

Marlene Matthews lives here, they

have families kids grandkids, kill

them all, let Nikki out she is your

only hope she will get the job done

son, I will be watching out for you,

let me do a locator spell to find

Marlene Matthews we will start with

her first, her kids grandkids and

great grands we will kill them all, If

Toni really loved you son, she would

not have went along with him so easy for get her son, we will take the kid when the time is right, no worries, no one knows I am alive, so they will have no idea who or what is behind the massacre. Nikolai are you sure this is what you want? Because once we start there is no looking back, if we have to go round for round with Matthew, I will face him I am stronger then you, give me a hug son, let Niki out so we can get started. Niko hugged his mother then went to the bathroom to take a shower, change and transform into Nikki. Little did Niko or Kaitlyn know Nikki had a plan of her own and being turned into a vampire was number 1 on her list of thing to get done, Nikki knew she was strong enough to face pastor if she had to, Nikki had plans to kill Brittney and Toni along with Thomas for not completing the job, Nikki knew once she had vampire power to add to her own, she would be able to face pastor if needed, Nikki planned to raise her child with Toni on her own, she finished in the bathroom

and went to the kitchen where

Kaitlyn was fixing dinner, hello

mother said Nikki, Kat turned

around to see Nikki looking like a 19

year old version of herself, my

beautiful daughter Kat said and

kissed Nikki, mami I need to make a

run I will return before dawn, Child

of mine where are you going? To see

an old friend Mami she kissed her

mother and switched out the door,

leaving a seductive scent behind,

she turned heads wherever she

went. Nikki was on her way to see
an old vampire friend name
December, who she once loved and
he loved her, she knocked on the
door and he open it, he grabbed her
and they kissed for what seem like
forever, he picked her up and took
her straight to his room, the made
love for hours, Nikki told him her
plan and asked him to turn her into
a vampire and he did, she also
asked him to help her raise her baby
once they took it back, he agreed he
loved Nikki and he was as powerful

as pastor and as old created by the same entity, she knew with December on her side she had a chance, she didn't want to put her mother in harm's way, December and Pastor were old friends that grew up together. Nikki decided to wait a year before her attack on Pastor so he would think she just let it go for now she would watch from afar and plan her revenge, she change her whole appearance and changed her name to Angela Lewis, so Pastor had no clue who she was,

December changed his name to
Ralph Lewis and changed his
appearance as well they moved to
DC to watch, joined the church and
just waited, the first thing on
Nikki/Angela's list was Thomas, but
he was nowhere to be found, so she
befriended Toni in church one
Sunday they became the best of
friends. Nikki/Angela finally decided
it was time to make her move, she
would kill Toni and take the baby,
while Ralph killed Brittney,
Angela/Nikki invited Toni and Baby

out for lunch, she compelled Toni to give her thc baby and to then jump out the window while the car was moving fast on the busy highway. Brittney was on her way home with little Matthew, she pulled into the drive way and her and the baby got out walking the short way to the door, as Ralph walked up on her thinking he could compelled her to give him the child and kill herself, what he didn't know is she had been taking Vervain, which made her poison to a Vampire and un-

compellable, she sprayed him with
Vervain pastor had made for her,
Ralph immediately started burning
and ran off, but not before
snatching the baby. Brittney had no
chance she called Pastor
immediately, she went inside to wait
for Matthew to come, she cut on the
TV and on the news, Toni jumping
out a moving car, it said nothing of
the baby, Pastor bust through the
door, Brittney started to scream he
took my baby Matt! I don't know
who he was but he tried to compel

me, I sprayed him with the Vervein, hc snatched Matt and ran, I just watched Toni on the news, she is dead, she jumped out the car while it was moving, they didn't mention her baby, what the fuck is going on Matt!? Nikolai! I will take care of this; everything will be fine.

Angela and Ralph met up and left DC headed for Africa, Angela was upset that Ralph didn't kill Brittney but please he did get the baby little Matthew, they sat on the plane smiling please with what they pulled off, happy the plan worked,

Pastor went straight to Nikolai

mother, he bust through her door

and he threaten her to call Nikolai

now! I want my kids, or I will kill

you right now! He said, she called

Niko Angela answered they just got

off the plane, Kat said baby I'm

calling to say goodbye Matthew is

here its my time, she hung up the

phone and started to use her magic

on Matthew, it took all she had, but

she did it he passed out and then

she passed out using all the energy

she had left in her, she died to save her son. Nikolai called his friend Lord to go check on his mom, Lord went and found Matthew and Kat both passed out, Lord worked his magic and brought Kat back, she was weak but alive, he buried Pastor in the back yard, he should have burned the body and cut off the head because pastor is not dead, but they would soon find that out the hard way.

Sasha/Tina/Brittney

/Kelly

After a long wait and no return Brittney and Kelly teamed up to find Pastor, they also became lovers, Kelly turned Brittney into a Vampire and there whole life mission at the present time was to find Pastor and Baby Matt, Brittney knew what Ralph looked like she was determine to get her baby back and Husband no matter what, with Kelly on her side they would search until found they both love that man, Brittney called Sasha and told her what happen and she came back to DC to help find her father, between Sasha, Kelly Tina and Brittney they would find Pastor and bring him home soon, Sasha said to the ladies let's take a trip to New Orleans I need to pay Kat a visit. Who is Kat asked Brittney, Nikolai's Mother? My heart is telling me he is there, she is very powerful and can read minds, so control your thoughts around this old Witch, looking like she 25 but

she is 210-year-old lets go.

The Lewis

Ralph and Angela and the kids landed safely in Africa, Ralph had a house already in place, they were looking forward to their new life, the Lewis's and there kids Darren Lewis aka baby Matt and Chelsea Lewis Toni daughter lived happy for 3 years in Africa until one day, Darren came home from school and said he met his aunt Sasha, and that's all he said, they packed up that night and left, they moved to Paris, now fearing that their life of lies would be ruin by the truth, they were in love with the kids and this new life and would do whatever they had to, to protect it, it was a knock at the door Angela open the door and there standing in front of her was Brittney and Sasha with Kelly standing right behind them, Angela face turned red, she couldn't believe who was standing in front of her right now, the kids weren't home so she let them in, Ralph walked in the room and seen the ladies and was shook and ready to go into attack mode,

they all sat quite for a minute, then

Angela said what can I do for you

ladies if you are looking for Niko he

is dead. Sasha said now you know I

know right? Stop playing with me

Nikki, Niko whatever the fuck you

call yourself now, where is my

father?

To be Continued..........

I am Author Angela Joy Clemons, Writer, Director, Producer, this is part 2 to The Secret Kiss, please enjoy and spread love. Anything is possible if you believe.